Florence K. Upton

The Adventures of Two Dutch Dolls and a "Golliwogg"

I0639953

Outlook

Florence K. Upton

The Adventures of Two Dutch Dolls and a "Golliwogg"

1. Auflage | ISBN: 978-3-73262-147-7

Erscheinungsort: Frankfurt am Main, Deutschland

Erscheinungsjahr: 2018

Outlook Verlag GmbH, Frankfurt.

Reproduction of the original.

The Adventures of two Dutch Dolls and a "Golliwogg"

by Florence K. Upton

Illustrated by Bertha Upton

'Twas on a frosty Christmas Eve

When Peggy Deutchland woke

From her wooden sleep

On the counter steep

And to her neighbour spoke,

"Get up! get up, dear Sarah Jane!

Now strikes the midnight hour,

When dolls and toys

Taste human joys,

And revel in their power.

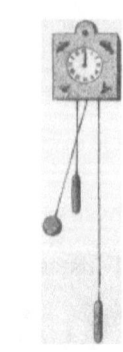

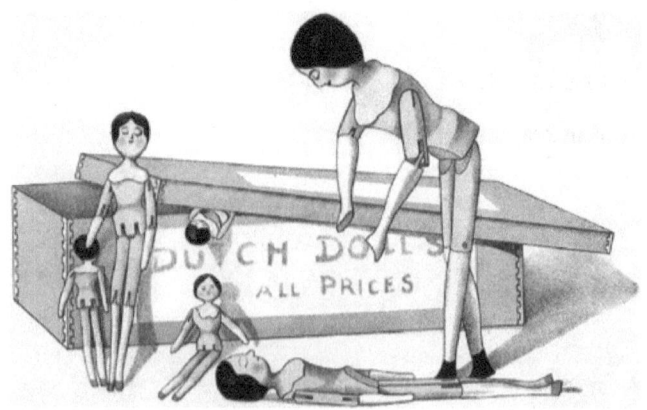

I long to try my limbs a bit,

And you must walk with me;

Our joints are good

Though made of wood,

And I pine for liberty.

For twelve long months we've lain in
here.

But we don't care a fig;

When wide awake

It does not take

Us long to dance a jig.

But who comes here across our
       path,

In gay attire bedight?

    A little girl

    With hair in curl,

And eyes so round and bright.

Good evening Miss, how fine
      you look,

Beside you I feel bare;

    I must confess

    I need a dress

If I would look as fair.

On that high pole I see a flag

With colors red and blue;

    Dear Sarah Jane

     'Tis very plain

A climb you'll have to do.

You're young and light—so now be
       quick

Dear sister good and kind;

    You look dismayed

    Don't be afraid,

It's not so hard you'll find.

Then up the pole with trembling limbs,

Poor Sarah Jane did mount;

    She dared not lag,

    But seized the flag,

Ere you could twenty count.

Big Peggy gazed with deep concern,

And mouth wide open too;

    Her only care

    That she might wear

A gown of brilliant hue.

Now Peg' by instinct seemed to know

Where scissors might be got;

    The "fits" were bad,

    But then she had

No patterns on the spot.

Soon where the garments hurried on;

Sarah looked well in blue;

    Mirror in hand

    She took her stand,

While Peggy pinned her's through.

Said Peggy—"After
     work so hard,
I think a rest we need;
    Let's take a ride
    Seated astride
Upon this gentle steed."
Then simple Sarah Jane
     climbed up
Upon his wooden back;
    With tim'rous heart
    She felt him start
Upon the open track.

Ere long they knew that hidden there,

Beneath a stolid mien,

 Dwelt a fierce will.

 They could not still

They rode as if by steam!

Peggy held on with tightening grip,

While Sarah Jane behind,

 Having no hold

 To make her bold,

To screaming gave her mind.

"O Peggy! put me down I pray!

I ride in mortal dread!

 Do make him stop,

 Or I shall drop

And break my wooden head!"

E'en as those piteous words she spoke,

They struck a fearful "snag"

    Their grips they lost,

    And both were tossed

Upon the cruel "flag".

Their senses for a moment gone,

They lay in ghastly plight;

    Their fiery steed

    From burden freed,

Maintained his onward flight.

Then each in aching consciousness

Rose slowly with sad groans;

    Next faced about

    With angry shout,

Followed by tears and moans.

Each blamed the other for the fall;
Until, in gentler mood,
    Their hurts they dress,
    While both confess
The crying did them good.
A wooden crutch poor Peggy finds
To help her on her feet;
    Both solemn-faced
    Their steps retraced
To where they first did meet.

But sorrow's tears are quickly dried
With dolls as well as men.—
    A jolly crowd
    All laughing loud
(I think you'll count just ten.)
Mounted a little wooden cart,
While Peggy, brave and tried,

Got up in front

To bear the brunt

Of "Hobby's" mighty stride.

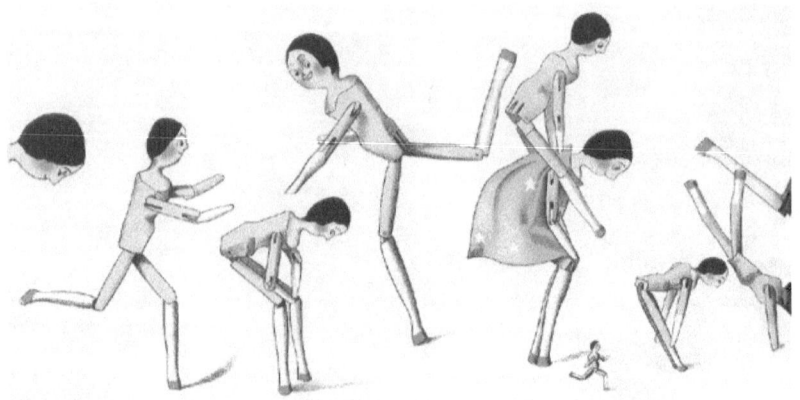

Finding a pleasant open space,

Gay Peg' unships her load;

    Suggests a game

    Which, it is plain,

Will soon be quite the "mode."

She tells of former Christmas nights,

When many of her kind,

    At leap-frog played,

    And merry made,

Fast running like the wind.

The happy moments swiftly sped

In unabated glee;

    Their lungs were strong,

    Their legs were long,

And supple at the knee.

But soon they hear the clock strike "two"
The hours are flying fast!

    With much to do

    Ere night be thro'

Its' pleasures overpast!
"Just one leap more!" cries Sarah Jane,
"This fills my wildest dream!"

    E'en as she spoke,

    Peg' Deutchland broke

Into a piercing scream.
Then all look round, as well they may
To see a horrid sight!

The blackest gnome
Stands there alone,
They scatter in their fright.
With kindly smile he nearer draws;
Begs them to feel no fear.
   "What is your name?"
   Cries Sarah Jane;
"The 'Golliwogg' my dear."
Their fears allayed—each takes an arm,
While up and down they walk;
   With sidelong glance
   Each tries her chance,
And charms him with "small talk".

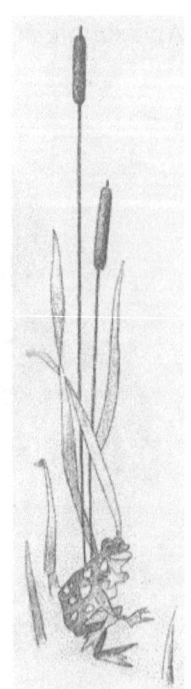

Another wonder now attracts

The simple Sarah Jane;

Upon one knee

She drops with glee,

In case this box contain

Some pretty thing to give her joy,

Some new-discovered treat!

Old Peg', who planned

The fun in hand,

Watches with face discreet.

The lock unlatched, the lid springs up,

Knocks Sarah on her back,

With flying hair

And trying stare,

Out of the box springs "Jack".

Our naughty Peg' enjoys the scene,

Laughs lung with fiendish glee;

Next takes to flight,

Gets out of sight,

Fresh tricks to plan you'll see.

Soon Sarah's heart
new
courage
takes,

She hits upon a
plan;

Makes up her

mind

To run behind

And kill the staring man!

Attempts are vain, he will not die!

In terror Sarah flees;

    Meets a new toy

    Called "Scissors Boy",

And begs him just to please.

To help her pay bad Peggy back

For her malicious tricks;

    Nor does she see

    That even he

Enjoys her woeful "fix".

Peg's pious face and peaceful pose

You'd think portended fair,

    When like a flash

    She makes a dash,

Sends Sarah high in air!

Entangled in the "Scissors Boy",

Alas! death seems quite near;

 Her trust betrayed,

 This hapless maid

Sobs out her grief and fear.

'Twas Peggy's fault the whole way through;

The boy had meant no harm.

 Both ran away,

 Nor thought to stay

Poor Sarah's fright to calm.

A handsome soldier passing by,
His heart quite free from guile,
  With martial air
  And manner rare
Soon helped the girl to smile.
He said the Ball would now begin
And begged her for a dance;
  She bowed so low,
  It looked as tho'
Her style had come from France.

A lively waltz the couple take,

While all admire their grace,

As round and round

Upon the ground

They spin with quickened
pace.

And shameless Peg' sits on a
chair

A true "flower of the wall"

While Sarah Jane,

Tis very plain,

Need never rest at all.

With graceful compliment the
     Clown

Bows low before the belle,

    Whose modest face,

    And simple grace,

In starry robe looked well.

"I know I'm but a stupid Clown,

And play a clumsy role;

    Yet underneath

    This painted sheath

I wear an ardent Soul."

Just then a jovial African

With large admiring eyes,

    Seizes her hand

    Just as the band

To give them a surprise

Strikes up the "Barn-dance"; like a flash

Both spring into their place!

    Away they go

    First quick, then slow,

Each movement fraught with grace.

The jolly pair then pause to watch

A "Magnate" from Japan,

    Who quite alone

    So far from home

(Poor harmless little man)

Dances a curious Eastern dance

To many a jingling bell;

    His brilliant dress,

They both confess,

Becomes him very well.

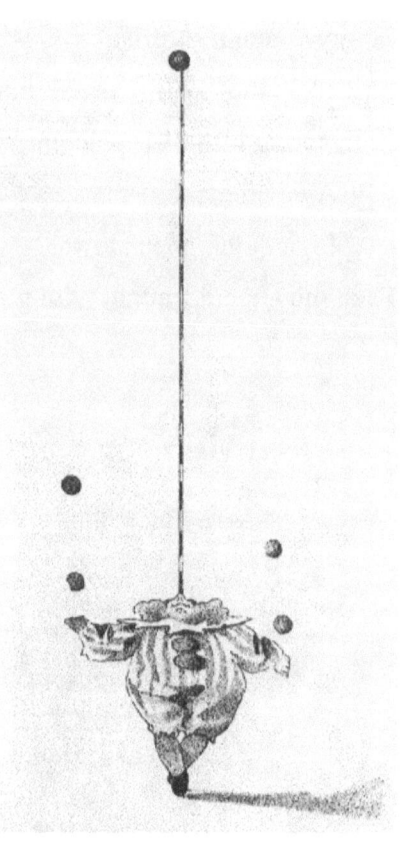

And now the Ball is at its
      height,

A madly whirling throng;

    Each merry pair

    A smile doth wear.

And Sambo sings a song.

While in their midst the artist
      head

Of "Golliwogg" appears,

    With Peg beside,

    Whose graceful stride

No criticism fears.

But even wooden limbs get tired
And want a chance of play,

So "Golliwogg"

A "jolly dog"

Suggests they run away.
The big shop door is bolted fast,
But through the yard behind,

Peggy has spied

One open wide,

Which she will shortly find.

A touch—A push—and out they fly

Into the starlight night;

    No one must know

    The way they go

They cover up their flight.

And though their laughing faces tell

How they enjoy the fun,

    No sound they make,

    But quickly take

Unto their heels and run.

Nor stop until they reach a field,

And find a lovely slide;

    No fear has Peg,

    But Meg and Weg

Cling screaming as they glide.

The "Golliwogg" with flying hair,

Takes the first lead you see,

Nor minds at all

The "Midget" small,

Her arms outstretched in
glee.

The sliders never dreamed of
    harm,

They sailed like ships at sea;

    'Twas Meg and Weg,

    Who Tripped up Peg,

And brought to grief their spree.

The wrong man often gets the
    blame

'Twas just so in this case,

    And balls of snow

    They madly throw

At "Golliwogg's" kind face.

He catches one in either eye,

And then turns tail to run;

    The steady aim

Of Sarah Jane

Grows very serious fun.

He does not like the way girls act,

For five to one's not fair;

There's no escape

One hits his nape,

Another strikes his hair.

"Vengeance!" he cries, "I'll pay them out!

If girls will play with boys,

There's got be

Equality,

So here's for equipoise!"

And then some monster balls he makes,

He does not spare the snow

And as each back

Receives a

whack,

Like ninepins down they go.

In life we have
        our
        "ups"
        and

      "downs",

These dolls enjoyed the same;

    Though down went Weg,

    Don't think, I beg,

'Twas due to Sarah Jane.

You see the sled was pretty full,

The hill was rather steep;

    Weg was to steer

    But in her fear

She took a backward leap.

Anon all reached the valley safe,

And skating longed to try;

    The ice seemed good,

    As each one stood

Upon the bank hard by.

While "Golliwogg" with cautious steps,

Toward the middle skates;

    They hear a crack!

    They cry, "come back

To your devoted mates!"

Too late! alas their call is vain!

He swiftly disappears!

    His kind forethought

    Is dearly bought,

It melts them unto tears.

But sturdy Peg is quick to act,

She gives an order clear,

    "Creep on your knees,

    And by degrees

We to the hole will steer."

They reach in time, Peg drags him out
With all her might and main;
    Poor "Golliwogg",
    A dripping log,
Must be got home again.
Behold sure signs of early dawn,
As down the field they start;
    A leaden weight,
    This living freight,
With faintly beating heart.

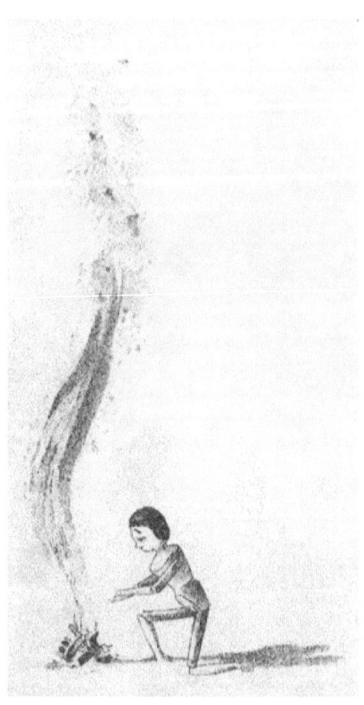

In half an hour the sun comes
up,

And shows a merry face;

He winks an eye

As passing by

He sees the skating place.

And when he peeps into the
shop

With jolly laughing eye,

Tho' he's not blind

He cannot find

A single toy awry!